P9-CLH-474

Andersen

JJ
(OVERSIZE)   Princess and the Pea

Millis Public Library
Auburn Road
Millis, Mass. 02054

Dedicated to
Hans Christian Andersen

JJ
oversize

Copyright © 1984 by Nord-Sud Verlag AG, Gossau Zurich, Switzerland.
First published in Switzerland under the title *Die Prinzessin auf der Erbse*.
Translation copyright © 1984 by Nord-Sud Verlag AG

All rights reserved. No part of this book may be reproduced or utilized in any
form or by any means, electronic or mechanical, including photocopying,
recording or by information storage and retrieval system, without permission
in writing from the publisher.

First published in Great Britain in 1984 under the imprint Abelard/North-South
by Abelard-Schuman Ltd. Reprinted in 1986 by North-South Books, an imprint
of Nord-Süd Verlag AG. First published in the United States in 1985 by
North-South Books. First paperback edition published in 1995.

Distributed in the United States by North-South Books Inc., New York

Library of Congress Cataloging in Publication Data
Andersen H.C. (Hans Christian), 1805-1875.
The princess and the pea.
Translation of: Prindsessen paa aerten.
Summary: A young girl feels a pea through twenty
mattresses and twenty featherbeds and proves
she is a real princess.
1. Children's stories, Danish. [1. Fairy tales]
I. Duntze, Dorothée, ill. II.Title.
PZ8.A542Pq 1985 [E] 85-7199

British Library Cataloguing in Publication Data
Andersen, H. C.
The princess and the pea
I. Title II. Duntze, Dorothée
III. Die Prinzessin auf der Erbse, *English*
839.8'1364 [J] PZ8

ISBN 1-55858-034-4 (trade hardcover)
12 11 10 9 8 7 6 5 4 3
ISBN 1-55858-381-5 (paperback)
10 9 8 7 6 5 4 3 2 1

Printed in Belgium

HANS CHRISTIAN ANDERSEN

The Princess and the Pea

Illustrated by Dorothée Duntze

North-South Books
New York

Millis Public Library
Auburn Road
Millis, Mass. 02054

APR 1 0 1995

There was once a Prince
who wished to marry a princess,
but she had to be a *real* princess.
He traveled the whole world over hoping to find
such a lady, but there always seemed to be
something wrong. There were plenty of princesses,
but whether they were real or not he just couldn't tell.
There was something about all of them that was not
quite right. So he came home again feeling miserable
because he wanted so much to marry a princess.

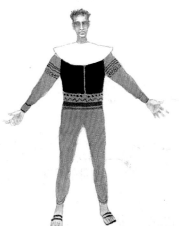

One evening there was a terrible storm; thunder rolled, lightning flashed and rain came pouring down. Then there came a loud knocking at the gate and the old King went down to open it.

A princess was standing outside, but goodness, what a state she was in! Rain was streaming down from her hair, dripping from her clothes and oozing out of her shoes, but she claimed that she was a real princess.

"We'll soon see about that!" thought the old Queen…

The old Queen spoke to the servants. "Go to the garden and fetch me a pea."

She took the pea, went into a bedroom, lifted all the bedclothes off the bed and put the pea under them.

Then she took twenty
mattresses, laid them on top of the pea
and then took twenty quilts and put
them on top of the mattresses.

This was where the Princess
was to sleep that night.

The next morning they asked the Princess how she had slept. "Terribly," said the Princess. "I scarcely closed my eyes all night. Goodness knows what was in my bed, but it was something hard and it's made me black and blue all over. It was dreadful!"

Now they could tell that she must be a real princess, because she had felt the tiny pea through twenty mattresses and twenty quilts. No one but a princess could be so sensitive.

So the Prince asked her to be his bride, for at last he had found a real princess.

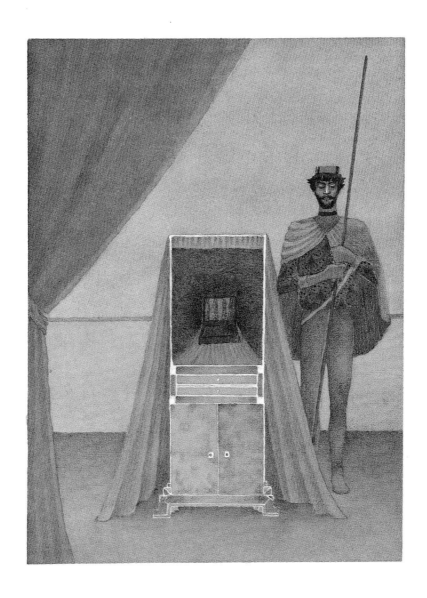

The pea was put in a glass case and is
there still unless someone has carried it
off. So you see, this is a true story!